Anthology After Eight

Richard Gillis

ISBN
978-1-8383095-0-3 (Paperback)
978-1-8383095-3-4 (eBook)

This is a work of fiction. Names, characters, places, and incidents either are the product of the author's imagination or are used fictitiously. Any resemblance to actual persons, living or dead, events, or locales is entirely coincidental.

Editing, cover art, and book design by PaperTrue Ltd.

Printed in Canada

First edition 2020

PROSE

The Stranger

If I, the Stranger takes away the barrier while breaking the heart of the bondholder

The spell will be cast on you and me, sealing our fate.

Table of Contents

Table of Contents

Connectivity 21ˢᵗ Century

Posting while I wheel my way down the Acadian coastline.

Messages and pics streaming into rockets aiming for the hole in the sky.

Knowing will fly to all, connection is all I seek for the sake of human contact.

It is the way of our time, trusting it will be the best way.

It is worth a try to find you. It is better than crying or even dying.

The connection I trust will be, you know failure to communicate will lead to a blackout. It is better than crying or even dying.

* * *

The Color Red

It flows in the veins and burns at the touch of the one you love.

Seeing red can be a burden if it unleashes the rage of no good intentions.

Red is my color of many colors.

Candy apples are fruits of honey sugar,

Red is the blush I have upon eating the forbidden fruit, join me if you dare to bare.

Wine is found in two colors: one is so, so, or more so, if you think white is memorable. Red is the color chosen by the Gods for health and romancing our body and soul.

Red is my color of many colors; I can see red when there is injustice flowing from my eyes, red in tearful episodes.

Run to the hills of green in search of peace, only stopping at the sign of red when justice has been fulfilled. Red is my sign of many colours.

So, as you express your view in favour or not of red, you must agree red is a color of strength. A color that will keep you in its protective shield as you kneel with the strength to kiss your color of choice to be found in nature's Spring Garden.

* * *

Loneliness

Loneliness comes upon us like the worst nightmare.

Sample of what we can all relate to sometimes in our lives.

"You enter a place of gathering, encounter others and quickly sense the negativity, recognizing that all do not value or care for your presence."

Loneliness can occur when all who see you recognize you as a common image of yourself in the mirror.

When it does occur that you find someone who can provide the warmth of physical touch, thus breaking the mirror image, you may withdraw, fearing rejection to come later.

Pray that you can again trust and love another, as love is all that is needed to bring back the "Will" to live.

Thus, I plead for the sake of others, who wish you no harm, only to love you in your presence today and tomorrow.

* * *

Not A Cross to Bear

Morning has arrived at 7:45 a.m. The house is heating up with the Sun's bursting elements. Slowly searching for my morning cup, will it be cool water or Jack Daniels on ice. Hopefully, it is not the latter, as Jack is not a friend of anyone.

By the way of my kitchen window, spring Sparrows in groups of two soar vertically to the sky followed by a curve to the ground in a repeated pattern with parallel fly by heading to their destination, a nearby tree. Home to be I am sure for the family of summer little ones to follow.

So, it is now Noon, I shake my thoughts of no concern out of my mind.

Blessed to still have the "Will" to live. Heaven has given me another day for me to share, *"Not a Cross to Bear".*

* * *

The Mirror of Your Mind

See the Reflection, the Mirror of your mind. Fly me there or take away my license to have a Soul. Can it be, we are easy to tease. Fly me there before you go. Lay me by your side so you can know of me for a time.

Friends knew of you; they are witness to the tight jeans moving in slow motion like waves in a slow-moving river.

Fly me there before you go, the rhythm of us will be until the reflection, the Mirror of your Mind has gone. Smile as you go, fly me somewhere you need not go.

* * *

Welcome to Sensitivity

The pain I have today is mine to experience. The pain of another is not yours to bear. You can volunteer for the sake of friendship to feel the pain by touch, to hold in your arms the other.

Whether you know me or not, we need to understand that you and I cannot accept our humanity if we choose to ignore our own painful events and that of our neighbours.

To accept our frailty means to seek help for ourselves and when required, provide the same to the members of our community, never stay in the bubble of me.

* * *

Simple Touch

Your touch when I talk makes my words fall by the way you are.

You are the star lighting the dark, giving life to my dying soul. Wonder you may, your eyes cannot tell a lie.

May the flowers bloom in your honour. Seasons come and go, and time cannot change what we have sown. Our eyes break their stare to see what is there.

A stranger I am no more. Gold and silver are gifts, they will not hold you, must accept the way you are.

* * *

Friendship Labels

A friendship can be close while at the same time distant. Thus, friendship may never bond into a physical relationship. The two accept the relationship as souls connected.

A friendship can be close as well as distant due to age and the barrier of having separate life journeys.

It may be the strongest and most everlasting one. It cannot be broken due to the strength of the two to hold its grip. The life journey of each may connect physically at a later time, chosen by the two. The only obstacle being one life ending their journey before the other.

Friendship can be one that grows parallel to one another. It may evolve into a physical relationship, even forever love, when there is a willingness to bond the parallel lives so they can touch and lock together.

* * *

I See So Much, Yet I See So Little

Poverty – Working Poor

Waking up to the same nightmare, the threat of homelessness, owing rent, the fridge is empty, counting change - can I buy anything for myself today?

Refugees

When others need us, only when we heed their cry will we come together and lift them to safety: providing food, shelter, and a helping hand.

Identity

First to be here from somewhere else, crying myself to sleep. Who am I? A shadow of once was me.

Colors of skin

Brown, Black, White, Sunburn, in-between colors, eyes tell the story within my color.

* * *

Moonlight Serenade (Not Really)

Try to run to the Moon
So soon, the cows need to moo
Milk me till noon.

See through the time of Youth
Until it is time to wish for final solitude.

Nick in time before I commit a crime
It is not worth a dime, only the thrill as is bouncing
you off the bed.

Sleep away your never naughty dream.

Your smile says it is a long time coming.

Chase the Buccaneer from port to stern until your
cleavage bows him to your command. Gold and
Silver is our goal, Pirates are told, for it is here for
us to enjoy as we are known to have no soul.

Time has come for your worth to be denied as you
turn to dust, part of Nature's way.

Stand up, hold your ground have your say if you want
to love me. It is better to be remembered that way.

* * *

Walls

Blocking my way, cannot go around nor climb to the other side. I must stay, live within here, searching for love by handing out paper roses.

What We Need Now: Love is what we have between you and I, Is it Enough?

One Human being is alone. Two make a pair. A pair multiplied builds a community. Multiple communities make mankind. When we are willing to be loved, supporting one another, the world becomes a wonderful place.

* * *

You Are Not Like Me

Broken heart, broken dreams as you break my arm so all can see you are not like me.

I was free to hug, play and work with whom I pleased until my rights were ceased.

A citizen called for my arrest, it matters not why or whether it is justified, you are not like me.

"Freeze, you are unlawful and, on the run," so you say, you are trained to force my compliance.

The curved metal bars around my hands you place. You have experienced that hands come in an assortment of colors.

It is your belief that you have the right to choose which hands will be locked and yours closed, soaked in leather sweat, for a swift flurry to ensure compliance.

I am told you are the citizen's righteous law and order man.

My plea for release only intensifies your smile of glee.

Commands you order are only interpreted as whispers in my mother tongue. You interpret my refusal as fear of intrusion into your authority.

Your voice will not be heard as you scream, "Let me go free, it is my home I want to be."

Broken heart, broken dreams, found tied to a lifeless tree, so all can see you are not like me.

* * *

Mon Cœur, My Heart

Mon Cœur et ton Cœur, Je t'aime aujourd'hui, demain, et toute ma Vie.

If you go, I will follow when Mom Dieu dit que c'est mon temps. Do not despair, we will find each other as a Heart that has only Love for you cannot be lost.

Mon Cœur et ton Cœur

Votre vie et ma Vie.

La monde crier and will not rest while our hands are parted for the needs of one and not the other.

When we are no longer, others will be there to bear witness of the Loving Heart.

Mon Vie et ton Vie.

La monde ne crier pas pour moi, Le Cœur vivant dans nous pour Éternité.

* * *

Just to be Young Again

I would like to turn back the clock or invent a time machine that can take me back where my life had heroes who were alive and well and just for kids like me: Lone Ranger, Davie Crockett, Zorro, Sky King, Roy Rogers and Trigger—just to name a few.

THRILLS consisted of a Ferris wheel and all food good was cotton candy and candy apples.

TRAVELLING TO FAR AWAY PLACES was taking the train to grandma's house.

GROWING UP was far in the future, and when I did grow up, I would be a policeman or better yet a Texas ranger!

GIRLS were weird!

SUNDAY MORNING church and turkey supper.

SLIDING DOWN MY FAVORITE SNOW HILL with a green handmade toboggan with my name *"Rickie"* carved into the front board.

COLLECTING marbles, rocks, coins, and comics.

WHO FOUND GOLD IN THE BACKYARD—I did! turned out to be *"fool's gold"* but still was gold!

MEMORIES ARE A TIME MACHINE—use it often and have a *happy smile-filled day*

* * *

My Guardian Angel

I LOST MY GUARDIAN ANGEL TODAY

I came into this world, kicking and screaming, my Guardian Angel was there to calm me, feed me and welcome me into this world.

I LOST MY GUARDIAN ANGEL TODAY

She was there to protect me, provide guidance, educate, share my joy and sadness.

I LOST MY GUARDIAN ANGEL TODAY

When all seemed lost and darkness set in my mind, she was there to bring me back to the heavenly light providing the love and strength to stay in the light and fight for what was right.

I LOST MY GUARDIAN ANGEL TODAY

GOD BLESS MOM

* * *

A Riverboat Dream

I dream of a Riverboat, painted a fire engine red.

I was one and ten when I would run to the shore to watch her coming up the line with Captain O'Connell blowing her whistle.

I am one and twenty now, living in a city that you and I will never know, searching for love within wallpaper and cement, but I still dream to this dying day of the Riverboat painted a fire engine red!

* * *

Sitting on the Sidelines

I sat on a cement railing as I do every day, observed a lonely ant busy at work, wondered what it would be like to be an ant for a day.

Before the thought had completed its journey, a stranger walked by and squashed it with his foot. I do not wonder what it is to be an ant anymore. Better to wonder about the purpose of Humanity.

* * *

The Creators

I sat and watched the Creators busy at work, changing the beautiful still waters into polluted sewage dumps.

The wild stallion changed into a four-wheeled monster.

The rich green fields changed into a four-lane highway.

I wondered where God had gone. Big brother had taken over!

There was no need for a God who created beautiful still waters, wild stallions, and picturesque wild green lands.

I watched the creators busy at work and said to myself: "What a tangled web we weave!"

* * *

The Cat Came Back

Stumbling next in line, "Coffee will take a minute, not much time for someone next in line. "Good morning–good afternoon, I mean" to the one who always serves with a smile and a twinkle in her eyes: "Where were you? You don't seem to know whether it is morning or afternoon."

"Well, I left on cloud nine, a stormy night, to let you know, where I met an angel sprinkling stardust. I stayed until it was time to go, leaving as I came, waking just now to my delight. I did not have a chance to notice the proper time to now greet another, not that it matters as long as the one I greet is you."

"You are like the cat that came back, stories of your roaming to be yours to tell as I interpret your state of mind: "Hello, I love you,' with a mischievous smile.

* * *

Cat Story

The cat came back from the Arctic shores of Baffin Island to the mighty Miramichi. He came back, you see, not as a hobo, just a cat.

He loves me so, from sea to sea, as he lays hugging his toy rat while purring next to my silly hat.

From my head to my pinky toe, I love him so!

A bow I place around his collar to remind him of home for next, he roams!

* * *

You Can Say I Know You

I came by an old friend today: "how do you do, the blues will always be close by, cannot be denied," says he. "Rightly so," say I, wait you say until the moon is blue to mention a lover's name. It has always been a haven for lost lovers.

The blues you say has no chains, it sets no time, may the blues be hidden to your delight when the stars appear tonight.

As I place silver and gold in the hands of those in need, I pray at the foot of Heaven's wishing well for a gift of love from you.

* * *

Can You See Me?

I was in grade nine, and she was in grade ten.

Her eyes melted my frozen body as she walked by in a cool and breezy form.

My soul was taken into her arms with a twinkle of her eye.

Can you say Hi before you say goodbye, I walked on by - lord have mercy!

* * *

Gennie

I know a girl, you know her too, Gennie is her name. She lives by the Bay.

I used to dream of her innocence from days gone by eager young men with doubtful intentions would ask to walk her home down by the Bay.

"You can learn a whole lot of wonderful things down by the Bay."

"Yes," she said one day and a whole lot of wonderful things she did learn. Now she runs from home to ask innocent young men to walk her home down by the Bay.

* * *

Expression of Love

Being in love has been expressed in words endlessly, but when all is said and done, what we have expressed from the time of our childhood gives the feeling of love "life" in the simple expressions of honesty such as: just wanted to say to you: "It is nice to see a bit of heaven before I lay my head down to sleep."

* * *

Emotional Probe

Autumn leaves, colors of the rainbow, hazel eyes; not what I have seen. Did think it through, but the road is still closed.

I am dying but do not know why.

Wish you were here but only in my mind's eye.

Stay asleep, snowflakes are falling. I am crying, but do not know why.

Am I bold enough to seek such a hold?

Can you tell me the meaning since my eyes are open?

Cannot be that hard to see through the clouds.

I am crying but do not know why.

The river flows by, knowing the reason why.

Tears are frozen. Wish for spring, tears will melt.

The river will flow, and you know why!

* * *

Nanook on the Tundra

What do you do when Nanook, the polar bear, comes to get you!

Stand and fight if you dare "Terror on the Tundra!"

Slippery as a seal, cunning as a fox, rage of a killer whale.

Nanook is going to get you. "Terror on the Tundra!"

You can stand tall, have a speed of full throttle. Snow machine—navigate by dog team—Nanook will outwit you: on the land, on the ice, in the water. "Terror on the Tundra!"

You can run like the wind, but before the day is done, Nanook, the polar bear, is going to catcha!

"Terror on the Tundra!"

* * *

1969 Flower Child

She sat so attentively in front of me.

I did not think much of her then.

I did not think much of anything. Then, years passed, and both went separate ways, but like a pierced arrow through a broken heart, I returned.

We talked and argued life issues until dawn, my eyes saddened, time had lapsed, the girl I knew was a woman now with eyes sparkling like the early morning mist, going in a direction not to be followed.

A figure at a distance watched, withered by life's storms but refusing shelter.

A whisper blew through the wind: "She sat so attentively."

"I didn't think much of her then, I didn't think much of anything then."

* * *

See You There

A dandelion, a red rose, and someone smiled.

The sun broke through the clouds today, lord.

Someone wants to die today.

"Not under my watch," says the spring flowers as a stranger smiles and hugs you until the will to live overtakes you. Happy days, the rains come, the flower gardens grew, and everyone knew why.

The sun broke through the clouds, a dandelion, a red rose, and the world smiled on this special day!

* * *

Spirit of Light

My heart beats with the spirit of light.

All your words—labelled as you state them to be are forgotten—drowning forever into the unspoken space of time.

My broken heart was to beat on long after, it was not meant to be.

Life in others will take up the spirit of light that is eternal in all of us.

* * *

A Music Box

A music box, a favorite of mine. Needs no words, just a sound of music, new or old, bringing forth memories and nothing more.

The glow of warmth, the healing of a broken heart; it is truly the voice of angels near yet so far.

Enjoy with thoughts of love for the one who chose you to receive such a small yet so magnificent a gift of love

* * *

North Star

I see **you** **and** **me** as the direct descendants of Adam and Eve, temptation being the electrifying connection between a man and a woman. We are clothed by God's command to be friends/partners but not to see or touch in our naked form.

What brought us to break God's command can only be attributed to Adam and Eve, who chose to touch and love in their naked form. By using what nature had given them, attraction, joy, happiness with lust mixed into the brew, allowed the birth of a new generation. It is God's way to forgive Adam and Eve for turning away from life eternal in Paradise.

The miracle of new life is not eternal but a temporary stay until another inherits the continuation of the miracle. In life, we also inherit *"Free Will"* and with it a choice to live in love and harmony or allow *"the Will"* to be lost in darkness.

May Darkness never be chosen, as it will destroy our *"Will"* to exist. Our only salvation is to seek and hold true to our hearts the Paradise of our Mother and Father. As our temporary stay ends, our Souls seek and find Heaven's eternal love hidden behind the *"North Star"*. It will always take you home if ever you find yourself lost.

* * *

Star Gaze

Wishing upon a *Falling Star* to the delight of my *Being.* The lady in your wish knows of the interest.

It cannot be as *the Mirror* cannot be broken, for it would surely shatter *Hope.*

The image is nature's physical beauty that is alive for the man and woman to see from time to time when God allows their paths to become one. Tears of sadness become tears of happiness for at least a moment until next time if another is granted.

* * *

I Do Not Want to Die Singing Alone

Serve with Honor

A soldier I am for my country. Both I and my fellow enemy cannot yield, just want to hold on to our oath, "Serve with Honor," even in the face of death.

Peace has finally come with my life spared. The military order arrived today for me and my fellow brothers to return home. My time of service has come to an honorable end.

* * *

Serve and Protect

To serve and protect, I chose for a time the honorable position of Constable in my hometown, accepting the risk of injury or death. Citizens who choose violence rather than accept my authority, so appointed by law, will choose their fate.

The time has now come that I no longer have the "will." My community and country must now search for another who has the heart and courage to serve.

* * *

Free Spirit

I now choose to free myself. A free spirit will be my time remaining to self-serve my body and soul.

You may now wish to call me the Aimless Wanderer. My claim to fame will be the love of adventure, leading to prospecting the Yukon Wild.

I, the penniless pilgrim, struck it rich and lost it all. What a time I confess to all who shared the raucous to its end at Molly's Pathway to Heaven.

Where I am now cannot be told, as I no longer have the means to communicate with anyone who may care, not one I could now name. As my final days are near, I plead my case to you now: "Please find the one I love!"

"I do not want to die 'Singing Alone'."

* * *

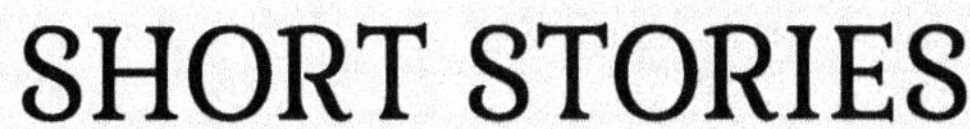

SHORT STORIES

Table of Contents

Story of Jonathan

Civil War 1861–1865

Background

Families were known to call it a war between brothers, as many chose to support the Southern versus the Northern states' way of life.

The Southern states saw it in specific terms, that is the North wanting to impose their way of life on them. Disagreements on tariffs and taxes resulted in the blockage of free trade of goods between states.

The Northern states believed that all men are equal, regardless of their color and therefore have equal rights as any man in front, beside or behind them in American society. The Southern states believed that Black men, women, and children were meant to be bought and sold for the purpose of work for the White man.

In summary, both sides wanted one country but could not agree on how it should be governed by all citizens. Thus, like any manly dispute, if you cannot settle a problem through words, violence erupts, which in this case was a civil war.

CIVIL WAR June/July 1863 Gettysburg

This was the scene of one of the most decisive and bloody battles.

The following are the facts of what happened to a person named Jonathan through the eyes of an unknown soldier in this epic battle.

Jonathan rose to the sound of cannon fire. The town's people were already up and standing outside, lined up on both sides of the street, including that in front of his family's house. He quickly got dressed and ran outside to the white picket fence. He watched the Union soldiers in their tattered blue uniforms and ghostly faces, including that of his older brother, marching by him.

His emotions tore at his heart. "Don't go, Michael," he screamed as his older brother turned to smile at him. The soldiers continued their march to the front line.

Sorrow, anger, fear, and love arose in Jonathan, a boy who, at that instance, became a man at 15 years. He ran back to his mother, pleading for her to let him go and join his brother, Michael, in the march.

His mother hugged him: "I need you here to protect our home and other mothers who no longer have partners." It seemed clear to Jonathan that staying here was not the way to protect them. He could not live with himself staying at home. So, when his mother went out of the back door leading to the vegetable garden, Jonathan ran through the front door and joined the march, being the last man to join the soldiers.

Late that evening, the soldiers rested in a field hidden inside a forested area. As the soldiers huddled around the campfire, roll call was sounded by the Registrar of Men and Recorder of Battles. All the men were accounted for except Jonathan, the blond freckled-faced boy with penetrating green eyes smiling in a devilish grin.

Jonathan, being under the age of 16 years and looking like thirteen, was stopped from travelling further until his brother found him sitting in his unit. It was he, Michael, who persuaded the Registrar to allow Jonathan to stay under his guardianship

The Field General, hearing of this from the Registrar, promoted Jonathan to the position of Drummer Boy. The job of the Drummer was to announce the commencement of the march to the battlefield. He always remained with the Field General at base camp. Jonathan would only enter battle if it was necessary for the Field General to lead the remaining soldiers to a fight to the last man.

Two days later, the fighting intensified as each hour passed and so did the casualties on both sides. On the morning of the third day, there was a break. Guns became silent, as both sides were desperately waiting for fresh supplies.

Whoever got their supplies first would be the first to attack. The soldiers on the Union side rushed to obtain their new provisions, ammunitions with a speedy return to the front.

It was well known from previous war experiences that soldiers should not be allowed much time to rest for many would ponder their fate, such as death, others would break down, while a number of them would do the unthinkable: desert. The decision was made by the Field General that he would lead a final assault; he ordered Jonathan, the Drummer Boy, to sound the drum. Before the start of this final assault, Jonathan had been notified by the Recorder of Battles that Michael had been captured or killed on the battlefield.

So, it began, the final slow, steady pace to confront the Southern Confederate Army. The Field General rode on a fiery white stallion, both of whom showed no fear due to previous battle experiences.

Jonathan never shed a tear, except for his mother. He marched proudly, sounding the drum in a manner that created a thunder that was easily heard by the Confederate Soldiers. As the sound of the drum came nearer and louder, the Confederate fired their cannons and soldiers fired their weapons, and many more soldiers began to fall to their death.

Metal fragments hit Jonathan in the back, shattering two or more of his ribs. Rifle pellets hit his leg and his right arm. The sound of the drum continued as Jonathan continued to beat it with his left hand. The sound began to grow quieter, slower, and then there was silence.

The Field General fell lifelessly followed by the horse collapsing alongside him. Jonathan, by instinct, went to his side.

A Confederate Soldier came over the hill, ready to finish the job when he froze upon seeing Jonathan's face. Private Timmy Jones recognized his childhood friend from an earlier time when both their families lived side by side in the same town and state.

Timmy began to cry, both hugged each other as a firing of a cannon below ended their lives, bringing peace to their souls.

Epilogue

Wars are hell on earth; upon their end, those who are left behind grieve the loss of their loved ones. We, the living souls, must resume our daily lives and educate the new generation of the horrors of war. We must teach them to strive always for love and peace in the world.

Honor those who have fallen! May God bless and care for them who now rest in heaven's field of honor.

* * *

Highway Wizard of Motorcycling

1967

Episodes riding my B.S.A. racing model motorcycle as they occurred from my memory.

Introduction

Comment by my next-door neighbor, Sexy Shannon, upon my purchase of the motorcycle, "Seventeen, a teenager with a death wish."

Driving at High Speed: A Car is stopped at the stop sign operated as I find out later from one of my high school teachers. My lack of attention does not allow me to stop, to avoid a collision, I popped a wheelie, driving up to the roof of the car. I pushed myself back down to the road. Dare I say, the driver got out of his car, ready to trash me for my irresponsible actions. I decided to pay my dues, took the punishment rather than being harassed in his class. It is noted we became friends in later years. The car was not damaged, cars back then were made with hardcore steel and relatively strong metals, not plastic, as is the norm with present cars.

Trips to Matapedia, Québec: Crossing the New Brunswick Border.

A well-known hotel had a shady, seedy tavern located at the back entrance that led to the basement. Patrons (except myself) were the toughest hombre in New Brunswick. Most of whom were seasonal workers whose lives were rough, having to scrape a living from day to day.

Why did I go there? Who knows for sure, other than I enjoyed their company and participated in the occasional brawl; win or lose, my buddies protected me from serious harm.

It is noted that my motorcycle was always hidden away from the parking lot to ensure it was not damaged or stolen by those so inclined to complete such an act.

I do remember my frightful parents who witnessed my appearance upon returning from one of these brawls. My excuses were many, one of the best was as follows: "I was beaten by a gang whose leader was enraged by his girlfriend flirting with me."

Acrobatics

It was not a surprise to my friends that I performed stunts with the motorcycle. I earned the nickname "Magic Christian".

One stunt I enjoyed performing while driving in the evening on Main Street or the Highway towards Dalhousie at a speed of 80 miles per hour was to stand up quickly on my motorcycle seat with hands in the air, then spread my legs to land back on the bike seat and take control of the handlebars. In some instances, I would lose control, going off the road and landing in the ditch or field area. Miraculously, there was only minor damage to parts of the bike such as foot pedals or handlebars. They were easy repairs at the local bike repair shop. I, of course, should have been seriously hurt, not this fellow, outside of a few scraps there was never a need to receive medical attention.

Motorcycle and Lawn Mower Race

My best friend and I were returning home. My parents were out for the weekend. I was warned that neighbours would be watching the home as well as checking up on me to ensure there was no hanky panky occurring in their absence. Thus, I complied with the order, "No visitors allowed in the house."

Upon arriving home late Saturday evening, my friend convinced me to play along with this fun activity. I started the motorcycle while he took the lawnmower from the side of the house, with some effort he started the old mower. The activity was to race up and down the street. We yelled. "1, 2, 3, go!" Yelling as we drove down the block. My next-door neighbor, Sexy Shannon, came out of her house, yelling as I drove up to ask her with a devilish smile, "What is the matter, did you have a bad dream?"

"Yes," she replied, "but see it is now real." Before I could start the bike again, she grabbed the key, ordered me back in my house, telling me not to come back out until morning. My friend sheepishly put back the lawnmower to the side of the house, proceeding quietly to walk home. If it was not for Sexy Shannon, we both would have been in a lot of trouble. Shannon never told my parents of the episodes while I was living at home, she waited until I left for university.

Late Summer Evenings

Driving out of the city limits taking dark country roads, I stopped to take off my clothes, putting them in my saddlebag. I then would speed down the dirt roads sometimes standing, naked as can be, quite a thrilling experience feeling free of all constraints.

* * *

Dream Sequence
May 2018

Walking up to an apartment building, I took an elevator to the top floor. As I got off the elevator, I noticed the windows in the hallway leading to the individual apartments. They were very narrow and rectangular as seen on train sleeping cars. The windows exposed the outdoor parking lot. The apartment doors were all open, I walked by the apartments until one caught my eye, several people were playing cards, laughing, and talking about their youth. I walked in and stated: "I cannot find my car in the parking lot, so I am lost and do not know where I am, please help me."

One of the men looked out of the narrow side windows in the hallway, then turned to me and said: "There it is, covered in branches."

I looked and said: "Yes, that is the car."

I opened one of the side windows and saw the tree was the same height as the narrow window. I squeezed myself through it, then grabbed onto the long branch. It bent under my weight all the way to the pavement. I walked to the car, removed the broken branches, checked the condition of the car, everything seemed operational.

I returned to the apartment building, went back up the elevator to the same top floor to thank the group for helping me find my car. It was not to be as the apartment door was locked. I continued down the hallway and found one door open, the following is what transpired as I entered the doorway to the apartment. Inside were five people behaving oddly with me. There was a couch on the right side of the wall, another couch on the L-shaped corner wall plus a chair next to it, a coffee table and a bathroom.

I began to scan the living room and saw a couple talking while holding hands. The wall with the coffee table next to the chair and the other couch stood a young blonde guy in his early twenties. He was standing on the coffee table banging his head on the wall followed by jumping onto the couch. He then returned to his chair, putting his hands on the wooden armrests. After observing everything, I leaned against the left wall closest to where I was standing inside the door. There, on the left, a beautiful lady was sitting in a large armchair like those in hotel lounges. Her hair was shoulder-length in the 1960s' style. I noticed she was staring ahead in the direction of the young man who had been behaving in an odd manner.

I was not noticed, and my sense all were ignoring my presence. The young man across the room begins to stand, I assume he would go through the same activity that I previously witnessed, thus I yelled: "Stop it". He looked at me and then sat back in his chair. He began to musically tap his hands on the wooden portions of his armchair and hum a musical tune. I looked towards the lady, the main figure in my dream. She also began to tap musically on her chair's wooden armrests. As I was about to say: "I recognize you", she began to sing a beautiful song with an angelic voice. The words are noticeably clear (unfortunately the words could not be retained by my memory). I continued to listen as the singing took a higher pitch, then I woke up, fearing, I assume, that I would be trapped forever in the dream sequence.

Dreams are very lucid and usually disappear from your memory upon waking up from your sleep. If you can remember, write it down for future review for possible meaning. It can be difficult to write about a dream, as dreams usually melt away before you can get the description on paper. I got lucky this time.

* * *

Lonesome Corner of the Page

I picked up my newspapers on the corner of Barrington Street, then moving to a nearby park bench, began the daily ritual of sorting papers for delivery to customers.

An old man who always sat on the nearby bench at the same time each morning would come over to sit and tell me stories of times gone by while I did my daily routine.

"You got a dime, Mister?" he would say knowing a little boy who enjoyed his daily stories would always find a dime somewhere for his daily coffee.

The old man loved to end his conversation by repeating the wonderful life he lived with Marie, his wife of 40 years.

"We met at a dance for military veterans. Her eyes and smile electrified him and, without hesitation, politely asked for her hand as his partner in the first dance."

The night exceeded all expectations, and not once from that night onward were, they ever separated in 40 years.

He would praise her at the end of his morning conversations: "Women were ladies back then, and Marie was the queen of them all".

"I was blessed; she chose me to be her servant and lover to the end of time."

Then, one day, the sun did not appear. The clouds burst into frozen tears. As I put on my winter coat, I noticed the old man, who always appeared no matter what the weather, was not sitting on the nearby bench.

It was September 4, 1967. My heart broke as I noticed on the back page in the far-right lonesome corner of the local newspaper, a death notice:

Charles Brown, unknown story of a life lived, found deceased in Room #210 at Barrington #2 Rooming House. No possessions of any consequences except in his hands a solid gold frame with a photo of an exceptionally beautiful woman signed: 'Marie to Charles, Angels and Lovers we will be on earth as it will be in Heaven.'

* * *

Raven

A misunderstood loner seeking acceptance during the midst of violence, most of it caused by his mistrust of people. Only Gail, his partner, had given him hope that there is a positive side to life.

His short-lived adult life came to a crashing end at age twenty-nine, ironically on his birthday.

Raven had dropped his guard when a visitor from a neighboring farm, who turned out to be the Devil disguised as his equal on the honor roll of a true patriot.

As Raven turned to open the door to welcome the visitor into his home, a sudden bolt of fire was heard by Gail who then witnessed Raven fall lifelessly to the floor.

His end came from trusting another, a single bullet entered his head, to lodge itself into Raven's wall of honor. The wall of honor showcased his military medals and letters of commendation from his superiors.

Gail was initially frozen to the dining room table; seconds later, she obtained the strength to stand and move towards the door where Raven lay in a pool of blood. She caught a glimpse of the assassin as he closed the door to the black limousine. The vehicle drove away, leaving dry dust of gravel floating in the air. So ended Raven's short life on earth.

The following is one of nearly a thousand calls to duty. The purpose of the mission described is to give a glimpse of Raven's secret classified life in the service of his county.

Case of the Dictator of Siam

The vintage 1952 Volkswagen van rattles to a stop.

An alarm sounded on Raven's Android phone. A deep breath was drawn which followed by complete silence, triggering his return to the role of Raven. By doing so, he left the programmed character of Johnny Stone, a potato farmer among many farmers in the small farming community of Sussex, New Brunswick.

The van stopped in a dusty road, sixty miles from John Stone's private rural airfield. A rural farm with a private airfield was essential for his profession as labelled on his confidential, private business card.

"Raven, Assassin will Travel"

An independent contractor with one employer

Secret Branch of the Canadian Northern Rangers

The next sound on Raven's phone was the theme of the Lone Ranger. His was a self-destructive #987 flip phone. When a two-sentence text message appeared, it would have to be followed by a thumb press by Raven. If not pressed, an automatic 10-second delay would occur, either way, the phone must be dropped to the ground. It cannot be held after the delay, as an acid capsule embedded inside the phone is ignited by a trigger activated by internal, pulsating sound waves.

Fire erupts and the phone melts into a black blob, no longer recognizable in its original existence as a phone.

Raven read the message after which he followed the instructions to drive immediately to his private airfield. On arrival, a Canadian Commodore helicopter landed and within seconds the helicopter hit maximum airspeed destination, Greenwood Airbase, Greenwood, N.S.

Upon arrival, Raven was escorted to a special briefing room inside the main hanger. The mission briefing was short on details as always, the precise details would be provided at the actual location by agents on the ground.

Raven left the hanger, completed a quick walk to his waiting Black Raven helicopter, all fueled and ready for take-off. A pilot trained to fly combat helicopters and latest fighter jets, friend, or foe, is one of his many skills which were appreciated for this type of profession.

The helicopter was equipped with custom-made air sound silencers. His flight coordinates were set on the flight panel. "Here we go," Raven yelled out to the Air Traffic Controller. Permission was granted to fly, and, within a few minutes, Raven had the helicopter flying at supersonic speed. The flight destination was a man-made Island under Canadian jurisdiction off the Coast of Jamaica.

Mission: Thunder Bolt

The military head/advisor to the President of the Republic of Siam, a puppet government was controlled by a Columbian drug/terror group with tentacles of control for its criminal behavior around the world.

The military board members provided the known details received from its agents embedded into the drug/terror group, "Canada has been targeted with multiple planned terror attacks involving explosions, poisonous gas, suicide missions in all major cities. We have identified and detained all known individuals, replacing them with our agents so as not to jeopardize the mission. If successful, we would permanently shut down this group, causing the authoritarian government to be toppled. Local popular leaders will take over to form a Canadian-style Federation".

July 2nd – 1 a.m. Mission Activated

Raven flew to the remote location by Stealth Black Hawk Helicopter where Agents Blacky and Rosebud were present to meet him. There was a two-hour long walk through dense bush to reach the target area. Upon arrival, the agents stated that they could not go any further. Raven was provided with two wrists watches: one with a GPS site location of the target and the other encoded with directions back to the location of the Black Hawk helicopter.

Raven had a maximum two-hour time frame, any longer would result in being abandoned to his own resources. In either case, the mission must be successful. He knew his life was expendable if the mission failed. Success was paramount to save innocent lives.

Before the agents departed, a backpack was handed to him. His special sniper rifle was inside the bag. The gun, fully assembled, had three barrels vertically set into the stock. One pull of the trigger discharged the three barrels at once. The first barrel had a silver bullet, the second contained a gold bullet while the third had a bullet-shaped explosive device that exploded upon hitting a solid object. The purpose of the final explosive device was to cause mayhem with ensuing fire and explosions. The chaos that would follow would allow Raven to casually walk away with a race to get back to the rendezvous place on time.

The Act – Shoot to Kill

The rifle was now in the hands of Raven with his GPS set to the location of the military headquarters on the outskirts of the city. The building was not secured fear of the military by the local citizens made it unnecessary for the military to have armoured security around the perimeter of the building. A vulnerability that Raven would exploit to his advantage. He arrived at the designated corner of the marsh. The location gave him a clear view of the corner window of the office and bedroom of Klaus, the military advisor to the Dictator, his intended target. The details provided by his agents were accurate to the tee. Raven's secondary watch was beginning to flash a white light, indicating it was about to be 4 a.m.; he had arrived with only two minutes to spare.

Klaus had a daily habit of opening the back-corner window to light his Cuban cigar. The open window allowed the smoke and smell to expel into the open air. This was done to please his girlfriend, Tash, who hated the smell of cigars.

The sniper rifle was assembled and ready to fire as soon as Klaus came to the window and lit his cigar. Raven's accuracy with his rifle was legendary. All he had to do was point the firearm in the direction of the target and pull the trigger.

On cue, Klaus came to the corner window, opened it, and lit his cigar. There was a quick pull of the trigger, discharging the ammunition in all three barrels, exploding Klaus's head and chest. The explosive device hit the inside wall instantly, turning the room into a ball of fire. There were screams and chaotic behavior from all present in the area, and this allowed Raven to dismantle his sniper rifle and place it carefully back into his pack. He activated the second GPS that had the directions set to take him back to the original rendezvous site.

He arrived at the site physically exhausted but with a clear mind. "What a wonderful day," Raven proclaimed as he nodded his head with a thumbs up to the two agents, thanking them for their service. The waiting helicopter fired up, and Raven took a quick run and jumped headfirst into the helicopter. The aircraft lifted and sped away with Raven yelling: "Hi-Yoh Silver away" to the pilot.

The helicopter soon reached its destination, the man-made island off the coast of Jamaica. Raven completed a mandatory briefing with the senior staff. After the briefing, Raven completed the return journey, ending where it started, at his rural airstrip.

It was now 7 a.m., back on home soil, and the sun was beginning to peek over the horizon. He casually walked to his waiting vintage 1952 Volkswagen. The vehicle struggled to start, but after a few tries, it came alive. A humorous smile appeared on Raven face, the first one in 48 hours. As he returned to his farmhouse, Gail, his beloved companion, greeted him with a forever hug.

Raven sat down next to Gail in his favourite leather chair. It was 9 a.m., and they both planned out the day, neither commenting, as always, on his disappearance in the last 48 hours.

It was Raven's last mission, as noted, at the start of this story. By 10 a.m., he was to meet and lose his life to the devil in sheep's clothing, who in a second of weakness he had trusted. Raven was the Devil's target with Hell, the final destination!

*　*　*

Taxi 1959

A memory

Yes, a memory that must be told, as my life as I have lived it, is owed to Taxi 1959.

A 1959 Chevrolet delivered to the Chev dealer in my hometown. A description always etched in my mind: painted yellow with chrome front to back with an interior of standard red felt seats with a red dashboard and ceiling to match.

Oldtimer Charlie fell in love with this beauty. The site of it confirmed his decision to open a taxi stand, the first and only taxi service in my hometown.

Taxi 1959 delivered a regular service route from Victoria street to Lansdowne to Roseberry on Main with late-night calls to all roads in between. He drove across the bridge from time to time for those needing a ride back home from sinful visits to unlicensed bars/hotels where the laws did not apply as in my hometown.

Oldtimer Charlie travelled the regular route as well as the unmapped roads in between, safely transporting customers to their home as well as visits to the local hospital for customers requiring emergency care. There were the secret customer-requested trips to local bootleggers after hours. Charlie knew them all, he paid no mind to the customers' need for such illicit beverages. They paid for the chauffeur service plus a tip to guarantee sealed lips.

Charlie's workday was a 14-hour shift most days with a shutdown on the Lord's day, Sunday. The taxi, known as #1959, remained loyal to Charlie for 30 years.

All knew Charlie's love for "Poppy", me, his adopted son in his mind. It was this love that allowed Charlie to willingly let go and transfer ownership of Taxi 1959 to "Poppy".

I, Poppy, was brought up by a family of five. The time came early for me to choose my path in life. As I remember, my Grade 10 homeroom teacher told me one day that I did not have the smarts to graduate from high school. Now, at 16 years of age, I was legally able to seek my independence. So, it came to be on that eventful day that I ran to the taxi stand as fast as I could go. I was greeted with a laugh and a nod of acceptance when I asked for a job. My mentor saw the mirror of himself in me, Poppy, the independent drive to be his own man.

I worked, cleaning the dispatch office, then on to the garage housing the one and only Taxi 1959. I was given the privilege to clean the exterior and interior of this gem of a car. My wages were meager, not enough to leave the family home. The day came when Charlie announced that his health was not what it used to be. Being a single senior, Charlie registered himself into the local "Windmills Nursing Home".

Before I go, Poppy, here are the City Licensing and transfer of ownership papers. Please sign here and here. We both went to the City Bureau and within an hour the taxi license and vehicle, named Taxi 1959, was transferred into my name.

The last drive for Charlie in Taxi 1959 was as a passenger with me, Poppy, in the driver's seat, beaming a glow only God could see at that moment.

I drove Charlie to his final stop, the Windmills Nursing Home. It is heartbreaking to tell you that Oldtimer Charlie died within the month due to age-related illness, so they stated. I knew it not to be so, Charlie's will to live ended when he no longer could serve his customers driving Taxi 1959.

Now, the time has come for the driver known as Poppy, at the ripe old age of 69, to retire for a final rest before Heaven's Gates opens for his own turn for eternal rest. Until that time comes, Taxi 1959 will rest in a specially built heated garage next to his one-bedroom bungalow on Victoria Street. There, you will see a license above the garage door with a sign reading "Final home of Taxi 1959".

Here, I write and declare the following code of conduct for those who choose a career in the Taxi Industry as passed on to me from Oldtimer Charlie.

* * *

Taxi Code of Conduct

Always be in uniform, clean at all times with extras to spare.

Polite, courteous, and honest.

Emergencies, medical or other, so deemed by the driver, the fare is waived.

All conversations are confidential unless criminal offences have occurred. The driver is duty-bound to report such to local authorities, bootleggers exempted.

Obey all traffic rules.

Maintain a medical emergency kit to be placed under the driver's seat.

Last but not least: "No Hanky-Panky" in the back seat, the driver is a God-fearing man.

* * *

Tragedy at Peggy's Cove

The Cove is situated on the shore of St. Margaret's Bay, Nova Scotia. There are many stories about how it got its name. The most popular, and the one chosen for this story, is as follows: a popular legend claims that the name came from the sole survivor of a shipwreck at Halibut Rock near the Cove. Many claim that she was a little girl, too young to remember her name; so, the family that adopted her called her Peggy. The young lady, in her adulthood, married a resident of the Cove in 1800 and with her local fame became known as Peggy of the Cove. Her story spread, attracting visitors from far away who by word of mouth named the village Peggy's Cove.

Where does one go when shelter and life are taken by no fault of their own? Jack found it to be so on Monday, November 13, 2017.

Jack's story

Jack Kelly's lifelong home had been passed onto him by his parents, Francis Kelly, and Monique Lapointe. As an only child, there was no dispute on who would get the house and its antique furnishing. The home was located two miles east of the famous lighthouse in the small rural community named Peggy's Cove.

A self-employed carpenter and part-time fisherman, Jack, unlike his buddies on the bay, refused to leave for work in Alberta. His love for Peggy's Cove and the family home was stronger than the riches of Alberta Oil.

Life in the community of Peggy's Cove was heaven on earth to him. It was more so than ever after his childhood sweetheart, Amanda Savoy, accepted his hand in marriage. Less than a year later, a beautiful baby girl named Chloé April Marie Kelly was born to the delight of the new family.

Life was complete in Jack's eyes, although he hoped, with a twinkle in his eyes, that Amanda's lovemaking would allow for at least four more children, regardless of gender.

Tragedy Strikes

An unanswered telephone call at 9:00 a.m. followed with a voicemail message: "Mr. and Mrs. Jack Kelly, this is I.C.E. Bank's Mortgage Division in Toronto, Ontario".

"We are notifying you, on behalf of the local branch in St. Margaret's, that your mortgage payments have not been rendered as per the mortgage contract, leaving us no choice but to initiate foreclosure proceedings. A sheriff officially acting on our behalf will ensure delivery of a letter verifying this decision along with an order to vacate the home within seven days."

The above action occurred due to Jack taking out a second mortgage to pay for a life-saving, non-insurable surgery instrumental in saving Amanda's life. The bank refused to re-negotiate mortgage payments for a three-month period to allow Jack to complete a housing contract. The value of the contract exceeded a year's mortgage payments.

It was a Saturday and Jack woke up at 10:00 a.m. to find Amanda absent from her side of the bed. His heart raced uncontrollably as he searched the house in a futile panic-stricken effort. Amanda was not in the house. He sat at the kitchen table in silent prayers before calling neighbors for help to locate her.

Before Jack awoke from his deep sleep, Amanda had risen and dressed in her running attire. The extreme weather patterns that year had the week's temperature ranging from 2 to 20°C, causing the winter ice, which was already fragile, to crack in large chunks and float away from the shore of Peggy's Cove. The warm temperatures also brought strong southerly winds and high waves smashing into the shoreline.

She did this early-morning ritual of a two-mile hike to the lighthouse every day since they got married. What was different this time was that Amanda had left the house for her daily walk an hour before sunrise, rather than the usual 8 a.m. and not before waking Jack for his shower and preparing a light breakfast of hot oatmeal and black coffee.

Arriving at the lighthouse, she would always kneel and say a prayer. That morning, Amanda waited at the lighthouse until the sun rose above the horizon, then she knelt and said her normal prayer. A few minutes later, Amanda stood up and, with a tearful stare in her eyes, ran to the dangerous, slippery, dark, rocks of the water's edge.

There, she waited patiently, leaning forward to meet the next hypnotic monster wave to pull her within its permanent grasp.

She justified her action to end her life believing the $500,000 life insurance policy would payout for accidental death, allowing financial stability for Jack and their daughter to survive and continue with life's journey.

One year passed; the insurance policy for accidental death was paid out by the insurance company leaving Jack and Chloé the financial stability to hold the family together. Jack and Chloé are broken with the loss of a wife and mother, knowing each must bear their own pain for this loss.

The insurance funds allowed Jack to build a new four-bedroom house on the main street lot within the village boundary of Peggy's Cove. Jack now has a boat touring business catering to Canadian, American, and European tourists. Chloé operates a glass and pottery shop, producing and selling handmade gifts of her own as well as other villagers' creations. Their lives are and forever will be tied to Peggy's Cove

* * *

Snowy's Adventures

Prologue

The following story is fictional. The characters, Snowy and Gail, are based on real people. Their attraction to each other was immediate, neither inquired about the other's background. They lived their normal lives in the moment to the very end.

Out of respect for them, no background information on their individual lives has been provided for this story.

At the Beginning – 1984

Episode 1

The night, as cruel as it was, allowed a full moon to shine through, exposing the vulnerability of a shadowy thin man who walked into Tim's Café. As he reached the counter, Gail, working at a distance, turned in his direction and with a smile spoke: "Hi, kind of a rainy night."

The shadowy figure named Snowy responded, "Yes, that kind of night." Snowy received his coffee and turned in Gail's direction and smiled, leaving as he came, into the darkness.

Several weeks after meeting and developing a close relationship with Gail, the unthinkable happened. Snowy left Chatham without a word to Gail about his departure. He left on a military aircraft with six other men, arriving at 2 a.m. in Resolute Bay, N.W.T. The team was escorted immediately to the Briefing Room at the Base Command Centre.

Snowy's Secrecy

Snowy was part of a Special Forces Division code name, Shandar, for the last 20 years. His missions took him to various locations in Asia and Central America.

The Mission

It was revealed in a briefing room that Snowy's mission would take him to Cartagena, Columbia. He was to depart in 24 hours after orientation and training was completed.

Background of the Mission Cartagena is a colonial city on Columbia's Caribbean Coast. It is famous for its castles, culture, history, and colourful buildings.

Cartagena played a major role in Columbia's history, protecting the country from several invasions as well as repelling pirates who desired the city's treasures.

December 21st

As scheduled, Snowy's aircraft landed at the public airport in Cartagena. He quickly began to move about, visiting shops and enjoying the casino nightlife to blend in with the vacationing tourists from around the world.

December 22nd

Snowy's Columbian contact, an employee at the Canadian Embassy, met him at the hotel for breakfast, then both left with a group of tourists on an antique, barely-running bus that took tourists daily to the mountain top that oversees the city. The trip allows tourists to visually experience the beauty of the whole city and in the countryside. The bus stopped at the designated spot whereby all its occupants departed to view the landscape. It was a short 30-minute stay; it was noticed that the military police were there as well to protect the tourists from being robbed or kidnapped by local gangsters or rebels.

"Time is up," the driver ordered everyone back to the bus so that they could continue to the next tourist attraction. One seat was empty; Snowy's contact quickly hid the empty seat with baggage. Snowy was left in the parking lot, and the local military police pointed to Snowy, ordering him to proceed on foot into the dense jungle environment.

The walk into the dense jungle was a struggle, although a cleared walking path did exist for a short distance. At the end of the walking path, Snowy was confronted by a group of men armed to the teeth. They immediately directed me to follow them further into the dense jungle.

Five hours later, Snowy arrived at the Rebel Camp Post. The Rebel Group has been known for 20 years as A.R.C. The group consisted of deserters of the Columbian Army as well as their family members. The women and children also received military orientation, training to increase their strength and survivability as Columbia's most feared rebel group. The group had one aim: to overthrow the Columbian government and establish a socialist government like that of Cuba's Castro Regime with ties to the Russian Soviet Republic.

Why was Snowy Here Now?

The Mission to do so had been assigned by both the Columbian Secret Service and our own Canadian Service Agency. Snowy's role in this mission was to act as a peacekeeper in the first tense negotiations for peace offered by the Columbian government to the A.R.C. Rebel Group.

It was 4 p.m., December 22nd, the A.R.C. Rebel Commander, known only as Zeppa, listened through his translator to the details of the Columbian Government Peace Agreement. The agreement, already signed by the Columbian President, only needed the rebel Commander's signature to begin the process of disarmament and reintegration of rebel forces back into Columbian society. The process was estimated to take three years to complete. It was a complicated process, as it included turning over their arms to the government. It would be done individually by each rebel and in return, each member would receive amnesty plus a financial award to transition back into civilian life for themselves and their families.

December 23rd

It was a marathon session completed at 6 a.m. on that day. The Commander signed the document. I placed the document in my common tourist type bag. The rebels who had escorted me to the location quickly marched me out of the area back to the original edge of the walking path that led me to the parking area. The Columbian military police were waiting and wasted no time in placing me in a presidential bulletproof vehicle. The next hour found me in the office of the President of Columbia, sitting next to the top Canadian and American diplomats for Columbia relations. Debriefing followed with the transfer to the President, the official peace treaty agreement now signed by both the President and the Rebel Commander of A.R.C.

This mission was successfully concluded, no time was wasted; arrangements were made to return me to home base. I boarded a military aircraft at 11 p.m. for my return flight to Resolute Bay, N.W.T., arriving on December 24th at 2 a.m.

Upon completing further debriefing at the Base Command Centre, Snowy quickly boarded the chartered aircraft taking him back to Frobisher Bay, N.W.T. Upon arrival, he was driven to his apartment where he changed, packing a new suitcase of civilian garments. He rushed back to the airport to catch a waiting aircraft. The charter was carrying him and another man back to the airport in Chatham, N.B.

Thoughts during his flight to Chatham

Snowy could only think of Gail working endless hours at Tim's Café. He did not know that Gail's thoughts were always about what she had done to drive Snowy away from her life. During the flight, Snowy thought the journey would never end, he could no longer contain his emotions and began to cry and in a soft voice said: "I am not leaving you; I could not tell you why I was leaving Chatham without an explanation. I told the Northern Commander in Resolute Bay that this was my last mission.

"You will also be pleased Gail that I have given a written intention to the local realtor in Chatham, stating my wish to purchase a home. It is located past the golf course, a wee down before you reach Stewart's Motorcycle Shop. The house has been on sale for two and a half years, causing the owner to finally reduce his price for a quick sale rather than let it sit empty for another brutal winter."

Snowy suddenly returned from his thoughts to the present as he landed at the airport in Chatham, N.B. He quickly picked up his suitcase and headed to his Hummer that had been sitting in a lonely state for his return from another completed adventure. Snowy drove to his apartment on General Manson Way. The apartment was small but had all the essentials, including a comfortable twin bed.

December 25th – Christmas Day

Snowy had slept for 15 hours due to his jet lag, waking up at noon. He spent the day watching television and preparing supper and returned to bed at 9 p.m. Christmas was not celebrated by Snowy, a single worn-out man. At least that is how Snowy thought of himself, and his attitude towards the holiday was similar.

December 26th – Boxing Day

A beautiful sunny cold day of -20°C greeted Snowy who awoke alert and ready to move ahead with his plan, starting with returning into Gail's life. He was always more comfortable in dealing with relationships in the evening. It was more romantic and easier to succeed in seduction.

Snowy walked quietly into the coffee shop, wearing a black business suit with a yellow tie to shield him from the weather elements. As he approached the coffee counter, Snowy's face glowed with excitement for there stood Gail, frozen in shock and unable to speak, with tears of joy flowing gently down her face. At that moment, Snowy could not contain his emotions as he gently lifted Gail over the counter, placing her in an embrace that burst with an energy that can only be found between those in love. There was no need for words, as each knew they could not live without the other.

There was little delay after parting from their embrace, as Gail placed the closed sign on the glass doors. It was closing time, and the place was empty except for the two of them. Next, Gail completed her duties to ensure all things were ready for the morning 6 am shift. Snowy in the meantime waited patiently in the corner booth by the glass doors. It was 1 a.m. when both walked out together, the doors were securely locked.

Snowy escorted Gail to his military Hummer only issued to special operations personnel in the Canadian military. "It was a gift from a friend," he quickly responded to Gail's curious expression on seeing the vehicle.

The coffee shop where Gail worked was two blocks away from Snowy's apartment on Vancouver Crescent. She had been on duty since 6 a.m. and unfortunately was required to stay until closing time. It was

11:55 p.m. when Snowy had chose to walk into the coffee shop. It was precisely the same time he had initially left with the final, "Goodbye, see you later, Gail."

Gail was expecting Snowy to drive her home even though she knew he had no idea where she lived in Chatham.

"Where are we going? You haven't even asked for directions to where I live." Snowy replied: "We are going to our new home on the river. The beautiful yellow house you always told me about, your dream house."

As they approached the house, Gail's eyes and mouth opened wide; there was a large sign with beautiful yellow flashing lights positioned at the front of the driveway with a simple message:

"Welcome home, Gail and Snowy"

A child was born to them a year after they settled in their new dream home overlooking the mighty Miramichi River. The boy named Jacklightning, a name picked with Gail's blessing of a Snowy comic book hero.

Life's dreams and wishes for both Snowy and Gail were now complete. Unfortunately, as we all know and have experienced, life is not a Disney dream come true. Tragedy is always lurking around the corner for each of us. Some of us will experience the ultimate, and it is so devastating that it destroys the survivor's will to live.

It was now the second year of Snowy and Gail's life together as a family. A winter storm was forecasted to hit the Miramichi region on the coldest day so far this winter, February 20th, 1992. Snowy was on his way out to pick up some emergency supplies, ending with a quick run to Timmy's for two large coffees to go before nestling in for the evening. "Love you, Gail and Jack," he had said, giving them a group hug before leaving to complete his errands.

It was thirty minutes since Snowy had left when a mysterious explosion was heard by all in the vicinity of the city business core. Snowy was just leaving the Canadian tire store when he heard the explosion. His heart began to race as if it knew what had happened due to the explosion.

He quickly headed back to his vehicle, speeding off to return as quickly as he could to his home. As he approached, his car came to a screaming halt due to a roadblock closing traffic a hundred meters from his home. Local police and firefighters were on the scene of the explosion. Constable Davis, recognizing Snowy, walked up to him, asking point-blank: "Was there anyone at your home?"

Snowy responded: "Yes, Gail and my son, Jack, were home."

Constable Davis, with tears in his eyes, "Come with me," As they both silently walked over to the site of the explosion.

Their dream home was destroyed, leaving in its wake ashes and twisted metal. The fire crew had found Gail and Jack burnt beyond recognition, placing both in body bags.

The ambulance staff placed the bodies in their vehicle for transportation to the morgue located at the Miramichi Hospital. Autopsies would be required before releasing the bodies for burial.

Snowy accepted the bodies were indeed that of Gail and Jack, the only love he had ever experienced was now gone. He had no interest in seeing the remains of his family. Snowy's identity along with his will to live ended that night.

It was apparent that after a private funeral attended by Gail's remaining family members, a brother and two sisters, Snowy had no life left in him. What followed was a voluntary admission to a mental health facility in a neighbouring town, serving residents of New Brunswick. He was diagnosed with having a nervous breakdown with suicidal tendencies. He was placed on a twenty-four-hour suicide watch for the first month.

Following a six-month stay, the medical professionals on-site deemed Snowy well enough to be released back into the community. Upon his release, Snowy drove to a monastery located in Rogersville. He had stayed there previously to meditate and come to grips with his occasional bouts of depression and general anxiety. During his stay, Snowy spent time working during the day with the monks at their dairy operations, followed by evening prayers and silent meditation.

After a month, during a stormy, rainy day, he heard a knock on his door. It was Joseph, the ninety-two-year-old monk. Upon entering, Snowy waived the monk to sit in one of the two chairs next to the window overlooking the courtyard.

Joseph began his conversation: "You know, Snowy, I am ninety-two years old, and the reason I have lived so long with my many sorrows, including the loss of all my family members, can be found within the walls of this monastery. My soul became one with God. The light I greet each day is goodness with sprinkles of love whether my mind and body treat me badly on any given day. Now, Snowy, what I have observed and am determined is your soul does not belong within the confines of these walls. Your true calling is to return to the Arctic from whence you came to greet and live on the land of the Inuit people. All your adventures, leading to saving thousands of lives in war-torn countries, originated and ended on that landscape. Leave and live out your remaining years in the land of the Inuit. Have a good night, Snowy." Joseph hugged him and moved towards the door, then turned and made the sign of the cross, closing the door.

Snowy cried himself to sleep, awakening to the sun with a smile on his face. He knew it was time for him to leave the monastery. Snowy packed his meager belongings and left his tiny room for the last time, going down two flights of stairs, turning right, opening the heavy wood door, leading to the dining room. Soon, the monks appeared after their morning prayers. A final hug was given to each one of the monks with a special long one to Joseph.

Snowy turned and walked out of the dining room to the main entrance door walking to the parking lot. His Hummer was there, covered in dirt and spider webs. He unlocked the door, turned the key, and the engine started without issues. He waved back at the monastery as he drove down the long courtyard, turned right, then sped down the main highway, heading back to the City Miramichi.

After visiting close friends, while staying at the Rodd Inn located minutes from the Miramichi River, Snowy left the inn early in the morning for a destination known to him, the Moncton International Airport. On arrival, he parked his car in the two-week parking area. He knew full well that the car will be found abandoned weeks later and be eventually sold at a car auction, as Snowy has no intention to return to New Brunswick. His first destination was a direct Air Canada Flight to Montreal, followed by a First Air Flight to Iqaluit, Nunavut. Here, he stayed overnight at the famous Frobisher Inn. The following afternoon, he took a direct Canadian North Flight to Resolute Bay, Nunavut. This is the community destination where his life began and would end.

A final tragedy, within a month of his return, took the life of Snowy, bringing peace to a broken man and a lost soul. It was March of a new year, a month of unpredictable weather where blizzards can form without warning, which is why no travellers on the land, experienced or not, should venture out alone in this frozen dessert, the Arctic Tundra.

Snowy's description of his final hours was found inside the lining of his jacket. He always carried a small pocket notebook and pencil in case of such an event described below.

"Lost my way on the Arctic Tundra. It is, I fear, below -50°C with a fading of the midnight sun. All who are alive and near, take shelter until the sun appears clashing with the northern winds."

I am hoping to find shelter, acknowledging now that my footprints leading right and now left will not lead me home. I rest my weary body against a pillow of stone. I dare to proclaim that it has not been disturbed since the birth of the planet earth. I plead for its strength to give me comfort, my eyes glistening with frozen lashes. The Northern Lights are crackling with the energy of God's power for all to see in this mysterious universe.

My body sits in a restful state as I contemplate my end. A prayer for a night of restful sleep with a dimming hope that the morning light will have by that time alerted the community that one of the Northern Rangers has not returned home.

End of Snowy's Journey

The Northern Rangers are true to their oath: "Do not rest until the ones you seek are found." So, it came to pass that the ranger found the one they were seeking at an unknown place on the ice that ended near the open water of the sea. Eyes were open wide with tears frozen and hands folded in prayer. All the rangers stood in a unified group, grasping hands: "Rest in peace, Snowy."

* * *

Born in Edmundston, New Brunswick, Canada, I completed my post-secondary education in Sociology and Psychology at Saint Mary's University in 1974. Further education constituted studying Public Administration at the University of Western Ontario. I was employed in public service for 30 years in the Northwest Territories as well as Nunavut Territory. I retired in 2011 and now reside in Miramichi, New Brunswick. This is my first publication of my numerous writings over the years.

www.ingramcontent.com/pod-product-compliance
Lightning Source LLC
Chambersburg PA
CBHW051006050726

47592CB00007B/2726